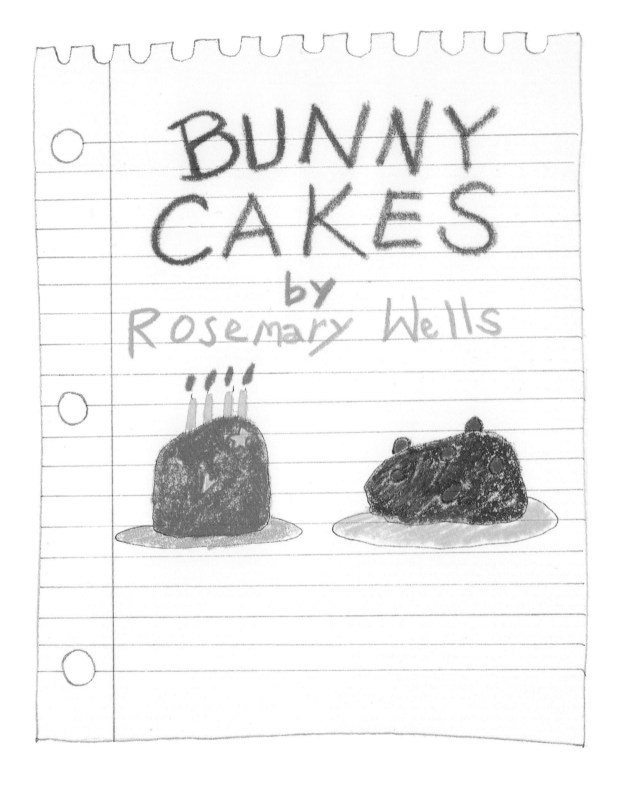

BUNNY CAKES
by Rosemary Wells

SCHOLASTIC INC.

New York Toronto London Auckland Sydney

For Ann Tobias

ISBN 0-590-23426-9

Copyright © 1997 by Rosemary Wells.
All rights reserved. Published by Scholastic Inc., 555 Broadway,
New York, NY 10012, by arrangement with Dial Books for Young Readers,
a division of Penguin Books USA Inc.

12 11 10 9 8 7 6 5 4 3 2 1   7 8 9/9 0 1 2/0

Printed in the U.S.A.
First Scholastic printing, October 1997

The artwork for each picture is an ink drawing with watercolor painting.

It was Grandma's birthday.

Max made her an earthworm birthday cake.

"No, Max," said Max's sister, Ruby. "We are going to make

Grandma an angel surprise cake with raspberry-fluff icing."

Max wanted to help.

"Don't touch anything, Max," said Ruby.

But it was too late.
Ruby sent Max to the store
with a list that said:

Max wanted Red-Hot Marshmallow Squirters for his earthworm cake. So he wrote "Red-Hot Marshmallow Squirters" on the list.

The grocer could not read Max's writing.

"Eggs!" said the grocer, and he gave Max eggs.

Max brought the eggs home to Ruby.

"Don't bump the table, Max!" said Ruby.

But it was too late.

Ruby sent Max back to the

store with a list that said:

This time Max wrote "Red-Hot Marshmallow Squirters"
in a different way.

Max hoped and hoped for his Squirters,

but the grocer still couldn't read Max's writing.

"Milk!" said the grocer, and he gave Max milk.

Max brought the milk home to Ruby.

"There's a yellow line on the floor, Max," said Ruby.

"You can't step over that line."

But Max crossed the line anyway.

Over went the flour.

Ruby got out her pencil.

This time Max wrote "Red-Hot Marshmallow Squirters" in the most beautiful writing he knew.

Max could almost taste the Marshmallow Squirters.

"Flour," said the grocer, and he gave Max flour.

When Max got home, there was
a sign on the kitchen door.
"Max, the kitchen is no place
for you," said Ruby.

Ruby finished up her cake.

She baked it and cooled it and iced it
with raspberry-fluff frosting.
"It needs something else, Max," said Ruby.

"Birthday candles, silver stars, sugar hearts,

buttercream roses," wrote Ruby.

Meanwhile Max had a brand-new idea.

BIRTHDAY CANDLES
SILVER STARS
SUGAR HEARTS
BUTTERCREAM
ROSES

He drew a picture of Red-Hot
Marshmallow Squirters on
Ruby's list and ran to the grocer.
He could not wait.

"Birthday candles, silver stars, sugar hearts,
buttercream roses!" said the grocer. "What's this?
Why, it must be Red-Hot Marshmallow Squirters!"

Ruby's cake looked just beautiful.

Max went out and put caterpillar icing on his earthworm cake.

Grandma was so thrilled, she didn't know which cake to eat first.

A MAX & RUBY PICTURE BOOK